Within the fairy-tale treasury which has come into the world's possession, there is no doubt Hans Christian Andersen's stories are of outstanding character. Their symbolism is rich with character values. From his early childhood in the town of Odense, Denmark, until his death in Copenhagen, Hans Christian Andersen (1805-1875) wrote approximately 150 stories and tales. The thread in Andersen's stories is one of optimism which has given hope and inspiration to people all over the world. It is in this spirit that the Tales of Hans Christian Andersen are published.

THE EMPEROR'S NEW CLOTHES
by Hans Christian Andersen
Translated from the original Danish text by Marlee Alex
Illustrated by Héléne Desputeaux
Published by Scandinavia Publishing House,
Noerregade 32, DK-1165 Copenhagen K, Denmark
U.S. edition 1987 by WORD Inc. Waco, TX 76796
Text: © Copyright 1987 Scandinavia Publishing House,
Artwork: © Copyright 1987 Toril Marö Henrichsen and
Scandinaviá Publishing House
Printed in Denmark by Aarhuus Stiftsbogtrykkerie
ISBN 0-8499-8535-8

The Emperor's New Clothes

Hans Christian Andersen
Translated from the original Danish text
by Marlee Alex
Illustrated by Héléne Desputeaux

WORD INC.
Waco, TX 76796

4

Many years ago there lived an emperor who was so very fond of beautiful, new clothes, that he spent all his money on his whim to be well dressed. He was not interested in his soldiers, nor in going to the theater, nor in riding in the great parks, unless it was in order to show off his new clothes. He had an outfit for every hour of the day, and just like the old saying, "the King is in his council chambers," it was said about the emperor, "he is in his emperor's clothes closet."

In the great city where he lived, there was a lot of festivity. Every day many strangers came to town. One day two crooks arrived. They pretended they were weavers and told everyone that they knew how to weave the loveliest cloth one could imagine. Not only were the colors and designs unusually beautiful, but the clothes that were sewn of the cloth had a remarkable quality: they became invisible for any person who either was not qualified for his position, or was unforgivably foolish.

"What nice clothes," thought the emperor. "By wearing them, I could recognize which men in my kingdom are not fit for their jobs. I would be able to tell the wise ones from the foolish ones. Yes, these clothes must be woven for me immediately!" He gave the two crooks much money so they could begin their work.

They set up two chairs before a loom and acted as if they were working, but there was not the least thing on the loom. From distant countries they ordered the finest silk, and the purest gold fibers, which they put in their own bag; and then they continued working on the empty loom. They worked on and on until very late at night.

"It's about time I find out how far they've come with the clothes!" thought the emperor. However, he was a bit anxious when he thought about how the person who was foolish or not fit for his job could not see them.

Now, he probably did not imagine he had anything to fear himself; but he could just as well send someone else first to see how it was going. All the people in the whole town knew of the unusual power the clothes were to have, and all were greedy enough to want to see how incapable or how foolish his neighbor was.

"I will send my old, honest prime minister to the weavers!" thought the emperor. "For he is the best one to see how the clothes are coming along. He is quite intelligent, and no one is more qualified for his position than he is!"

So the quaint old man went to the workroom where the two crooks sat weaving at the empty loom. "Bless my soul!" thought the old man; and his eyes nearly popped out of their sockets. "I can't see anything!" But he did not say it out loud.

The crooks asked him to step closer. "Isn't it a marvelous design? Aren't these lovely colors?" they asked. Then they pointed at the empty loom.

The poor old prime minister opened his eyes as wide as he could, but he could see nothing, for there was nothing to see. "Good heavens!" he thought. "Am I a fool? I would never have believed it; and not one person must know! Could it be that I am not fit for my job? No, it will never, ever do for me to say that I cannot see the clothes!"

"Well, why aren't you saying anything about it?" asked one of the crooks as he pretended to weave. "Oh, it's stunning! It's just exquisite!" said the old man, as he peered through his spectacles. "This design, and these colors! Yes, I shall tell the emperor that it pleases me very much indeed."

"Well, that's nice to hear!" said both weavers, and they began to describe the colors and the intricate patterns in detail. The old man listened well, so that he could describe it the same way when he came home to the emperor. And he did just that!

11

Soon afterwards, the crooks demanded more money, more silk and more gold fibers which they said they needed for the weaving. They stuck it all in their own pockets so that not a thread of it appeared on the loom and they continued, as before, to weave on the empty loom.

The emperor soon sent another of his old and honest advisors over to see how the weaving was going, and to find out if the clothes would soon be finished. The old man experienced the same thing as the prime minister had. He looked and looked, but as there was nothing to see, he could see nothing.

"Now isn't this a beautiful piece of cloth?" asked both the crooks as they pretended to display it and as they described the lovely pattern that was not there.

"I am certainly no fool!" thought the man. "Is it then my good position I'm not fit for? That's ridiculous! People will laugh; I must not let anyone know!" And so he praised the cloth he did not see and reassured them of his pleasure with the fine texture and the lovely design. "Yes, it is most exquisite!" he reported to the emperor.

All the people in town began to talk about the magnificent cloth.

And now the emperor himself wished to see it while it was still on the loom. Along with a large assembly of distinguished men, among whom were the prime minister and the advisor, he went directly to the two crooks, who were now weaving frantically without thread.

"Yes, isn't it magnificent?" asked both of the honest, old characters who had been there before. "Will Your Majesty be pleased to look here? Such a design! Such colors!" they exclaimed as they pointed at the empty loom, believing that all the others could, most likely, see the cloth.

"What is this!" thought the emperor. "I don't see a thing. This is frightful! Am I a fool? Am I not fit to be the emperor? This is the most dreadful thing that could ever happen to me."

"Oh they are very beautiful!" said the emperor aloud, "It has my highest approval." And he nodded in satisfaction as he studied the empty loom. He was not about to admit that he could not see anything.

The important men that he had with him stared and stared but they did not get anymore out of it than the others had, although they responded just as the emperor, "Oh, it is very beautiful!" And they advised him to wear the new clothes for the first time in the grand procession that was soon to take place in the city.

"They are magnificent!"

"Superb!" "Excellent!" it was passed from lip to lip. And with that, everybody was very well satisfied. The emperor gave each of the crooks a knight's medal to hang in their buttonhole, and the title of Royal Loomsman.

The entire night before the
procession was to be held, the
crooks sat up by the light of at least
sixteen candles. The townsfolk
could see they were busy finishing
the emperor's new clothes. The
crooks pretended to take the cloth
from the loom. They cut at the air
with big scissors, and sewed away,
using needles without thread. At last
they passed the word, "the clothes
are now ready."

The emperor, with his best court butlers, came straight away. Each of the crooks lifted an arm in the air, just as if he held something, and said, "See, here are the trousers! Here is the jacket! Here is the cape!" and so forth. "It is as light as a spider web! One wouldn't believe one had anything on, but that is the virtue of it!"

"Oh quite! Yes, indeed!" said all the court butlers. However, they could see nothing, for there was nothing to see.

"Would Your Royal Majesty now graciously be pleased to take your clothes off?" said the crooks. "Then we shall put the new ones on you over there in front of the big mirror."

The emperor laid aside all of his clothes, and the crooks acted as though they clothed him with each piece of the new ones which they were supposed to have sewn. Finally they wrapped him around the waist as if they tied something, which should have been the train; and the emperor turned and spun around before the mirror.

"My goodness, how well they suit you! How nicely they fit!" said everyone. "What design! What colors! It is an exquisite suit!" "They are waiting outside with the canopy which will be carried above Your Royal Majesty in the procession!" announced the Royal Master of Ceremonies. "Yes, well, I'm ready!" said the emperor. "Don't they fit well?"

And then he turned again in front of the mirror, for he wanted them to believe he was admiring his finery. The chamberlains, who were to carry the train, fumbled with their hands along the floor, just as if they were picking up the train. They walked along, holding the air, and dared not let anyone notice that really they saw nothing.

The Emperor's New Clothes

Explaining the story:

The story of the emperor and his new clothes will help us to be more aware of two basic problems which we all have: pride and fear. It is usually because of these two problems that we act foolishly toward one another. It often seems that the more important we are, or think that we are, the more difficult it is for us to be honest about our weaknesses. As in this story, the truth is finally told by one who has very little to lose, and therefore nothing to fear: a simple little child.

Talking about the truth of the story:

1. What did the emperor love more than anything else?
2. What does it mean to be vain or proud? How did this lead to telling lies, and trying to cover up the truth?
3. When the emperor tried to cover up the fact that he might be stupid, what happened instead?
4. What might have happened if the emperor were humble and honest instead of proud and vain?

Applying the truth of the story:

1. Can you think of a time when you might have tried to act important by covering up the truth?
2. Why is it foolish to try to act more important than we are?
3. Can you think of a special way to show your friends and family today that you think *they* are the greatest?